MISSING CAT

Must Find Duchy!!!

LOST

MISSY THE CAT
REWARD OFFERED

£2000 !!

Mi Mi is

LOST !!

MISSING

MOMO

LOST

REWARD

Missing

MISSING FROM BACKYARD

£4000 !

LOST CAT

REWARD IF YOU

REWARD

I WANT TO GO HOME !!

Ernie years male, 2 old

LOST GREY MALE
CALL 413589

LOST!!!

BIG BLACK CAT
WITH TWO WHITE TEETH !!!

~LOST~

LOST

HAVE YOU SEEN Muesli?

HELP FIND!

£2500

HAVE YOU

FOUND HER?

MISSING

OUT

CAT!

MISSING

CAT!

HE DISAPPEARED

LAST NIGHT...

MISSING

CURLY TAIL

HAVE YOU SEEN Our CAT?

Our dog is missing her!

LOST! ~ £££ REWARD

PLEA

LOST KITTY

LOOK AT THESE CATS!

REWARD 3000

To Toni, Harri and Charlie ~ M.R.

To all the cats in this book:

生奶冰

Happy、Amber、高麗菜、王大吉. Face、阿咪、露姬、花花、吳妮妮、Neo、阿肥. Charcoal、廖妞妞、王咪咪、胖胖、Qtt、Chubby、王岱萌、摸摸. 小D。、湯圓、白雪. Cofe、楊妮妮、小安. Amy、巴特、小胡弟、Choco、老咪咪、小咪、樂樂. 蔥花、紅豆、阿蓮. Soap、Mumu、王雪飛、陳咪咪. 芋粿、張小樂、Sally、駑收. Muesli、Ernie、Goofy、小乖咪、決決、咪吉、張咪咪、鳥咪、趴米. 阿呆. 南寶、奶油、歐歐、金金、Pussy. Tora、小葵、萌萌、小金鋼、咪嚕、卡栗、khaki、貓咪. 瞎瞎. 髒髒、乖乖、阿蒲、阿笨、Pandalin. 綠油精、喇咪、芭樂、Klavier. Two、O₂、Maoma 呂小皮. 小不黑占、豆子、三三、花花、雷弟、光復路、忌廉. tttt. 苣苣、小叮、搖頭、該該. Miken、小豆姜、柚子. Momo. 張有為、毛弟、菲毛毛、Fubo. 龍龍、罨罨~C.L.

First published 2019 by Walker Books Ltd, 87 Vauxhall Walk, London SE11 5HJ · Text © 2018 Michelle Robinson · Illustrations © 2018 Chinlun Lee

The Pawed Piper

Michelle Robinson   illustrated by **Chinlun Lee**

WALKER BOOKS
AND SUBSIDIARIES
LONDON • BOSTON • SYDNEY • AUCKLAND

I wanted a cat to cuddle.

A great big furry fluffball,
like the cat in my book.

So I laid a trail.

Balls of wool and
ribbon ...

saucers of milk ...

tiny balls
that jingled ...

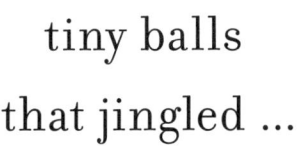

and soft cushions.

Now, what *else*
did cats like?

I called in on my gran.

She said that
Hector liked catnip,

cardboard boxes

and helping to read
the newspaper.

I borrowed some things.

Then, I waited...

But no cats came.

Not even a kitten.

So I took my book to bed,
and hugged that instead.

Then something
woke me up.

Something purry,

something furry,

something warm

and soft

and cuddly...

"Hallo, Hector!"

"Oh, you brought a friend.
And another ... and another!

ALL
THE
CATS!"

Five, six, seven, eight ...
nine, ten, eleven...
I lost count at
SIXTY SEVEN!

Fat ones, skinny ones,
massive ones and mini ones.
Cats with spots and cats with stripes.
Grumpy cats with scowling faces,
playful ones that chased my laces.

All day long,
just me and my cats, cuddling.
It was wonderful.

I loved them all.
Especially the cat who made herself
at home in my sock drawer,
and wouldn't come out.

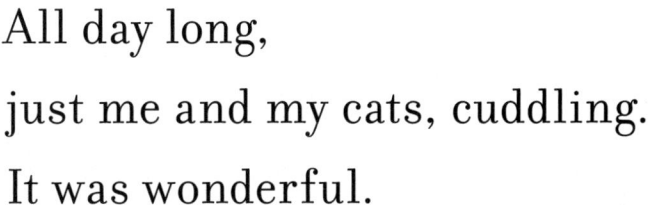

But when I went to take
Hector home...

"Oh, no!"

I didn't mean to take
anyone else's cat,
I just wanted one
of my own.

Gran said I had to give them back.

ALL THE CATS.

It wasn't fair, everyone else had a cat to cuddle.

Me? I just had my book.

Although...

I'd forgotten about the cat in my sock drawer.

She'd been so quiet.

And now I knew why...

ALL THE KITTENS!
Black ones, cream ones,
somewhere-in-between ones.
Each with tiny paddy paws
and perfect elfin ears.

I loved them *all*,
and I looked after them
until it was time for them
to go to their new homes.

All except the smallest one,
who had made himself
at home in the corner
and wouldn't leave...

Not ever.

We lost HER!

FOUND

PLEASE CALL US

~HELP~ FOUND

We want to go home

ATTENTION,

Missing Cat Contact us

FOUND!

FIND MARMIE & PEA

FOUND

MISSING CAT

"FOUND"

REWARD OFFERED

SHOW ME THE WAY TO HOME

FOUND

LOST

FOUND

MISSING FOUND

LAST SEEN

REWARD £2000

Lost Cat.... please bring our Mae home!

FOUND

LOST

FOUND!

SOCKS STEALER

LOST LULU

FOUND

She is sleepy all the time

LOST PET

FOUND

Daisy

LOST CAT

FOUND!

COULD BE HIDING CALL IF SEEN!

LOST MALE CAT

FOUND

3 LEGS

FOUND

SOCKS STEALER

IF YOU SEE HIM

FOUND

PLEASE CONTACT

Please Return FOUND!

↑ He eats a lot everyday.

MISSING

FOUND!

Maggie

IF YOU SEE ME

PLEASE TAKE ME HOME

FOUND

MISSING FROM GARAGE!

FOUND

HE LOVES FOOD REWARD

We are looking for her!

FOUND

HAVE YOU SEEN HER?

LOST CAT!

She is Cali

FOUND

LOST Chubby Cat

FOUND

CALL immediately! 213387

HELP!!!

PLEASE FIND FOUND

LOST

FOUND!!

£1000 REWARD